D12976S9

YOURS AFFECTIONATELY, PETER RABBIT

Miniature Letters by Beatrix Potter

FREDERICK WARNE

First published in Great Britain by
Frederick Warne (Publishers) Ltd.
London, England, 1983

Reprinted 1983

ISBN 0 7232 3178 8

Printed and bound in Great Britain
by William Clowes Limited,
Beccles and London
D7167.983

Contents

Picture Sources

All the pictures in this book are by Beatrix Potter. The illustration which appears on the front cover and title page is a detail from a water colour drawing for her uncle, Fred Burton of Gwaynynog, near Denbigh, Wales, and was kindly made available to us by Mr. and Mrs. T. Smith of Gwaynynog. The picture on page 9 is from a greetings card design first published in *Beatrix Potter's Address Book*. Illustrations from the tales appear as follows: from *Peter Rabbit* on pages 10 (detail, *left*), 87 and 90 (detail, *above*); *Squirrel Nutkin* on pages 15, 16, 21 and 23 (detail); *Benjamin Bunny* on pages 13 and 44; *Two Bad Mice* on pages 29, 30, 32, 33, 35 (detail), 40; *Mrs. Tiggy-Winkle* on pages 41, 44 (detail), 46, 47, 58 (detail) and 90 (detail); *Pie and Patty-pan* on pages 25 (detail), 27 (detail), 65, 66 and 69; *Jeremy Fisher* on pages 49, 51, 55, 56, 61, 62 (detail) and 63; *Tom Kitten* on pages 78 (detail, *below*), 79, 80, 83 and 84 (detail); *Jemima Puddle-Duck* on page 81 (detail); *Samuel Whiskers or The Roly-Poly Pudding* on pages 36, 68 (detail), 71, 72, 73, 74 (detail), 76 (detail) and 85; *The Flopsy Bunnies* on pages 91 and 94; *Ginger and Pickles* on pages 37, 38, 39, 59, 77 and 82 (detail); *Mrs. Tittlemouse* on pages 17 (endpaper detail), 53 (detail) and 60 (endpaper detail); *Mr. Tod* on page 93; and *Pigling Bland* on page 14. Illustrations from *Peter Rabbit's Almanac for 1929* (republished under the title of *Peter Rabbit's Diary*) appear on pages 10 (endpaper detail), 11, 95 (endpaper details) and 96 (endpaper details). The illustration detail on page 12 is from a rejected picture from *The Tale of Peter Rabbit*, first published in *A History of the Writings of Beatrix Potter*; and the illustrations on the back cover and page 3 were first published in *Beatrix Potter's Birthday Book*. The miniature letters reproduced on page 6 are from the Leslie Linder Bequest at the Victoria and Albert Museum, London, and the illustrations on page 8 are from *The History of the Writings of Beatrix Potter*.

Introduction

To entertain some of her little friends, Beatrix Potter invented correspondence between Peter Rabbit and others of her famous characters, telling of their continuing adventures outside their tales. These miniature letters were probably written between the years 1907 and 1912. They were shaped so that they could be folded up into tiny envelopes with drawn-on stamps, and distributed—sometimes in a doll-size G.P.O. mail-bag or a bright red enamelled post-box—to the little Moores, children of Beatrix Potter's ex-governess, to Lucie Carr—the Lucie in *The Tale of Mrs. Tiggy-Winkle*—and her sister Kathleen, to John and Margaret Hough, Drew Fayle, Miss M. Moller, and the Warne children.

'You will find some curious correspondence in Louie's post office,' Beatrix Potter wrote to her publisher, Harold Warne. 'I am not sure whether it is rather over the heads of the children.' But Louie Warne, the little girl responsible for *The Story of A Fierce Bad Rabbit* because in her opinion Peter was 'much too good a rabbit', would have been heartened to read of Peter's daring plan for yet another raid on Mr. McGregor's garden, and would have appreciated fully Mrs. McGregor's dark reference to her 'new py-Dish' which was 'vary Large'.

'Some of the letters were very funny,' said Beatrix Potter. 'The defect was that the inquiries and answers were all mixed up.' One hopes that the Squirrel Nutkin letters to Old Brown arrived in correct order so that Nutkin's obsequiousness, increasing with his desperation to get back his tail, could be enjoyed. Imagine the build-up of suspense

Merry Xmas

Miniature letters
to Margaret Hough

Dear Miss Hough
If you please I'm
a very Merry
Christmas xxx

These are crackers!
With love I remain
Mrs Ti: winkle

Mrs Tabitha Twitchit
wishes
Margaret Hough
a Merry Christmas

Happy New
Year

from one letter to the next—until Old Brown's terse reply put an end to that tale!

Tom Thumb's begging letters to Lucinda Doll deserved an award for their sheer effrontery, and Drew Fayle's suggestion that Mr. Jeremy Fisher should be married sparked off some lively correspondence from that independent gentleman and from Mrs. Tiggy-Winkle who didn't see herself in the role of Mrs. J. Fisher at all. Other letters—of complaint—revealed that Mrs. T.W. was not the efficient washerwoman that her tale had led us to believe!

Christmas greetings to John Hough were echoed in some of the letters to his sister Margaret, but hers had illustrations too—often lightning pen-and-ink sketches of the senders. Examples are shown in this introduction.

Hitherto Beatrix Potter's miniature letters have appeared in the first two editions of *The Art of Beatrix Potter* and later in *The History of the Writings of Beatrix Potter*, weighty books, not easily accessible to children. This selection has been chosen to amuse—in a format 'small enough for little hands to hold', and illustrated with Beatrix Potter's illustrations.

True appreciation of the subtle humour in these letters depends very much on knowledge of the tales themselves. To get the most enjoyment from *Yours Affectionately, Peter Rabbit*, children should be familiar with *The Tale of Peter Rabbit, The Tale of Benjamin Bunny, The Tale of Pigling Bland, The Tale of Squirrel Nutkin, The Tailor of Gloucester, The Tale of the Pie and the Patty-pan, The Tale of Two Bad Mice, The Tale of Samuel Whiskers or The Roly-Poly Pudding, The Tale of Ginger and Pickles, The Tale of Mrs. Tiggy-Winkle, The Tale of the Flopsy Bunnies, The Tale of Mr. Jeremy Fisher, The Tale of Mrs. Tittlemouse, The Tale of Tom Kitten,* and *The Tale of Mr. Tod.*

ANNE EMERSON

My dear Duchess,

If you are at home and not engaged
will you come to tea tomorrow? but if you
are away I shall put this in the post and
invite cousin Tabitha Twitchit. There will
be a red herring & muffins & crumpets.
The patty pans are all locked up. Do come.
yr affect friend Ribby —

Beatrix Potter often varied the
wording of the letters, which she sent
to several children (see p. 66)

The mail bag made by Beatrix Potter

G.P.O

Peter Rabbit's Correspondence

Mr. McGregor,
Gardener's Cottage.

Dear Sir,
I write to ask whether your spring cabbages are ready? Kindly reply by return & oblige.

Yrs. truly,
Peter Rabbit.

Master P. Rabbit,
Under Fir Tree.

Sir,

I rite by desir of my Husband Mr. McGregor who is in Bedd with a Cauld to say if you Comes heer agane we will inform the Polisse.

Jane McGregor.

P.S. I have bort a new py-Dish, itt is vary Large.

Master Benjamin Bunny,
The Warren.

Dear Cousin Benjamin,
  I have had a very ill written letter from Mrs. McGregor she says Mr. M. is in bed with a cold will you meet me at the corner of the wood near their garden at 6 this evening? In haste.

       Yr. aff. cousin,
       Peter Rabbit.

Master Drew,
Kylimore.

Dear Master Drew,
  I am pleased to hear you
like Miss Potter's books. Miss
Potter is drawing pigs & mice.
She says she has drawn enough
rabbits. But I am to be put
into one picture at the end of
the pig book.

      Yr. aff friend,
x x   Peter

x x x x x   x x x x

Squirrel Nutkin's
Correspondence

Mr. Brown,
Owl Island.

Sir,

I should esteem it a favour
if you would let me have back
my tail, as I miss it very
much. I would pay postage.

Yrs. truly,
Squirrel Nutkin.

Mr. Old Brown Esq.,
Owl Island.

Dear Sir,

I should be extremely
obliged if you could kindly
send back a tail which you
have had for some time. It is
fluffy brown with a white tip.
I wrote to you before about it,
but perhaps I did not address
the letter properly. I will pay
the postage.

Yrs. respectfully,
Sq. Nutkin.

Old Mr. Brown Esq.,
Owl Island.

Dear Sir,
   I should be exceedingly
obliged if you will let me have
back my tail, I will gladly pay
3 bags of nuts for it if you
will please post it back to me,
I have written to you twice
Mr. Brown, I think I did not
give my address, it is Derwent
Bay Wood.

            Yrs. respectfully,
               Sq. Nutkin.

The Right Honourable
Old Brown Esq.,
Owl Island.

Sir,

I write respectfully to beg
that you will sell me back my
tail, I am so uncomfortable
without it, and I have heard of
a tailor who would sew it on
again. I would pay three bags
of nuts for it. Please Sir, Mr.
Brown, send it back by post &
oblige.

Yrs. respectfully,
Sq. Nutkin.

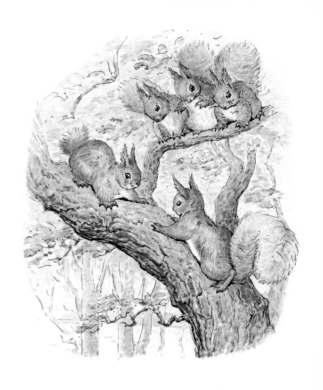

O. Brown Esq., M.P.
Owl Island.

Dear Sir,

I write on behalf of my brother Nutkin to beg that as a great favour you would send him back his tail. He never makes—or asks—riddles now, and he is truly sorry that he was so rude. Trusting that you continue to enjoy good health, I remain,

Yr. obedient servant,
Twinkleberry Squirrel.

Master Squirrel Nutkin,
Derwent Bay Wood.

Mr. Brown writes to say that he cannot reply to letters as he is asleep. Mr. Brown cannot return the tail. He ate it some time ago; it nearly choked him. Mr. Brown requests Nutkin not to write again, as his repeated letters are a nuisance.

Dr. Maggotty,
The Dispensary.

Dear Dr. Maggotty,
   Having seen an advertisement (nailed on the smithy door) of your blue beans to cure chilblains, I write to ask whether you think a boxful would make my tail grow? I tried to buy it back from the gentleman who pulled it off, but he has not answered my letters. It spoils my appearance. Are the beans very strong?

                    Yrs. truly,
                      Sq. Nutkin.

Sq. Nutkin Esq.,
Derwent Bay Wood.

Sir,
    I have much pleasure in
forwarding a box of blue beans
as requested. Kindly
acknowledge receipt & send 30
    peppercorns as payment.

            Yrs.
        Matthew Maggotty, M.D.

Dr. Maggotty Esq., M.D.
The Dispensary.

Sir,

   I am obliged for the box of blue beans. I have not tried them yet. I have been wondering is there any fear they might make me grow a *blue* tail? It would spoil my appearance.

                    Yrs. truly,
                       Sq. Nutkin.

Sq. Nutkin Esq.,
Derwent Bay Wood.

Sir,

   I do not think that there is
the slightest risk of my beans
causing you to grow a blue
tail. The price per box is 30
peppercorns.

Yrs. truly,
      M. Maggotty, M.D.

Dr. Maggotty.

Sir,
   I am sending back the box
of blue beans, I think they
have a very funny smell & so
does my brother Twinkleberry.

                    Yrs. truly,
                       Sq. Nutkin.

Lucinda Doll's Correspondence

Mrs. Thomas Thumb,
Mouse Hole.

Miss Lucinda Doll will
require Hunca Munca to come
for the whole day on Saturday.
Jane Dollcook has had an
accident. She has broken the
soup tureen and both her
wooden legs.

Miss Lucinda Doll,
Doll's House.

Honoured Madam,
 Would you forgive my
asking whether you can spare
a feather bed? The feathers are
all coming out of the one we
stole from your house. If you
can spare another, me & my
wife would be truly grateful.

 Yr obedient humble
servant,
 Thomas Thumb.

P.S. Me & my wife are grateful
 to you for employing her as
 char-woman I hope that she
 continues to give satisfaction.

P.P.S. Me and my wife would be grateful for any old clothes, we have 9 of a family at present.

Mr. T. Thumb,
Mouse Hole.

Miss Lucinda Doll has received Tom Thumb's appeal, but she regrets to inform Tom Thumb that she has never had another feather bed for *herself*. She also regrets to say that Hunca Munca forgot to dust the mantelpiece on Wednesday.

Miss Lucinda Doll,
Doll's House.

Honoured Madam,

I am sorry to hear that my wife forgot to dust the mantelpiece, I have whipped her. Me & my wife would be very grateful for another kettle, the last one is full of holes. Me & my wife do not think that it was made of tin at all. We have nine of a family at present & they require hot water.

I remain honoured madam,

Yr. obedient servant,
Thomas Thumb.

Mrs. Tom Thumb,
Mouse Hole.

Miss Lucinda Doll will be
obliged if Hunca Munca will
come half an hour earlier than
usual on Tuesday morning, as
Tom Kitten is expected to
sweep the kitchen chimney at
6 o'clock. Lucinda wishes
Hunca Munca to come not
later than 5.45 a.m.

Miss Lucinda Doll,
Doll's House.

Honoured Madam,
  I have received your note
for which I thank you kindly,
informing me that T. Kitten
will arrive to sweep the
chimney at 6. I will come
punctually at 7. Thanking you
for past favours I am,
honoured Madam, your
obedient humble Servant,

  Hunca Munca.

Messrs Ginger & Pickles—Grocers—in
account with Miss Lucinda Doll, Doll's
House

4 thimblefuls of brown sugar @ 2d   =   1 farthing

6   „   „ white ditto @ 2d   = $1\frac{1}{2}$ „

3 tastes stilton Cheese   @ 1/3 per lb. say $\frac{1}{10}$ farthing

                                            $2\frac{6}{10}$ farthings—

                                            $2\frac{1}{2}$d (about)

with Messrs G & P^s comp^ts & thanks.

Miss Lucinda Doll has received Messrs Pickle & Ginger's account, about which there is some mistake. She has lived for some months upon German plaster provisions & saw dust, and had given no order for the groceries mentioned in the bill.

Miss Lucinda Doll,
Doll's House.

Messrs Ginger & Pickles beg to apologize to Miss Lucinda Doll for their mistake. The goods were selected (& taken away from the shop) to the order of Miss Doll. But Messrs Ginger & Pickles' young man had his doubts at the time. The messenger will not be served again.

Mrs. Tiggy-Winkle's Correspondence

Mrs. Tiggy Winkle,
Cat Bells.

Dear Madam,
  Though unwilling to hurt
the feelings of another widow,
I really cannot any longer put
up with *starch* in my pocket
handkerchiefs. I am sending
this one back to you, to be
washed again. Unless the
washing improves next week I
shall (reluctantly) feel obliged
to change my laundry.

            Yrs. truly,
                Josephine Rabbit.

Mrs. Rabbit,
Sand Bank,
Under Fir-Tree.

If you please'm,
    Indeed I apologise sincerely
for the starchiness & hope you
will forgive me if you please
mum, indeed it is Tom
Titmouse and the rest of them;
they do want their collar that
starchy if you please mum my
mind do get mixed up. If you
please I will wash the clothes
without charge for a fortnight
if you will give another trial to
your obedient servant &
washerwoman,

              Tiggy Winkle.

Mrs. Tiggy Winkle,
Cat Bells.

Dear Mrs. Tiggy Winkle,
  I am much pleased with the getting up of the children's muslin frocks. Your explanation about the starch is perfectly satisfactory & I have no intention of changing my laundry at present. Nobody washes flannels like Mrs. Tiggy Winkle.

  With kind regards,
            yrs. truly,
            Josephine Rabbit.

Master D. Fayle,
Kylimore,
Co. Dublin.

Dear Drew,

I have got that mixed up
with this week's wash! Have
you got Mrs. Flopsy Bunny's
shirt or Mr. Jeremy Fisher's
apron? instead of your pocket
handkerchief—I mean to say
Mrs. Flopsy Bunny's apron.
Everything is all got mixed up
in wrong bundles. I will buy
more safety pins.

Yr. aff. washerwoman
T. Winkle.

Master D. Fayle,
Kylimore.

Dear Drew,
   I hope that your washing is
done to please you? I consider
that Mrs. Tiggy Winkle is
particularly good at ironing
collars; but she does mix
things up at the wash. I have
got a shirt marked J. F. instead
of an apron. Have you lost a
shirt at the wash? It is 3
inches long. My apron is much
larger and marked F. B.

                    Yrs.
                         Flopsy Bunny.

Mrs. Tiggy Winkle,
Cat Bells.

Mr. J. Fisher regrets that he
has to complain about the
washing. Mrs. T. W. has sent
home an immense white apron
with tapes instead of Mr J. F.'s
best new shirt. The apron is
marked F. B.

Jan. 22. 1910.

Mrs. Tiggy Winkle,
Cat Bells.

Mr. J. Fisher regrets to have
to complain again about the
washing. Mrs. T. Winkle has
sent home an enormous
handkerchief marked 'D. Fayle'
instead of the tablecloth
marked J. F.

If this continues every week,
Mr. J. Fisher will have to get
married, so as to have the
washing done at home.

Correspondence Concerning Jeremy Fisher

Master D. Fayle,
Kylimore.

Dear Master Drew,

I hear that you think that there ought to be a 'Mrs. J. Fisher'. Our friend is at present taking mud baths at the bottom of the pond, which may be the reason why your letter has not been answered quick by return. I will do my best to advise him, but I fear he remembers the sad fate of his elder brother who disobeyed his mother, and he was gobbled up by a lily white

duck! If my friend Jeremy
Fisher gets married, I will
certainly tell you, & send a bit
of wedding cake. One of our
friends is going into the next
book. He is fatter than Jeremy;
and he has shorter legs.

Yrs. with compliments,
Sir Isaac Newton.

Master Drew Fayle,
Kylimore.

Dear Master Drew,

I hear that you are interested in the domestic arrangements of our friend Jeremy Fisher. I am of opinion that his dinner parties would be much more agreeable if there were a lady to preside at the table. I do not care for roast grasshoppers. His housekeeping and cookery do not come up to the standard to which I am accustomed at the Mansion House.

Yrs. truly,

Alderman Pt. Tortoise.

Master D. Fayle,
Kylimore,
Co. Dublin.

Dear Master Drew,

In answer to your very kind inquiry, I live alone; I am not married. When I bought my sprigged waistcoat & my maroon tail-coat I had hopes .... But I am alone ... If there were a 'Mrs. Jeremy Fisher' she might object to snails. It is some satisfaction to be able to have as much water & mud in the house as a person likes.

Thanking you for your touching inquiry,

Yr. devoted friend,
Jeremiah Fisher.

Master Drew Fayle,
Kylimore,
Co. Dublin.

Dear Master Drew,
   If you please Sir I am a
widow; & I think it is very
wrong that there is not any
Mrs. Jeremy Fisher, but *I*
would not marry Mr. Jeremy
not for worlds, the way he
does live in that house all
slippy-sloppy; not any lady
would stand it, & not a bit of
good starching his cravats.

   Yr. obedient washerwoman,
        Tiggy Winkle.

Mr. Alderman
Ptolemy Tortoise's
Invitations

Mr. Jeremy Fisher,
Pond House.

Mr. Alderman
Ptolemy Tortoise

Request the pleasure of

Mr. Jeremy Fisher's
Company at Dinner
on Dec. 25th
(there will be a snail)

R.S.V.P.

Mr. Alderman Ptolemy Tortoise
Melon Pit,
South Border.

Mr. Jeremy Fisher accepts with
pleasure Alderman P. Tortoise's
kind invitation to dinner for
Dec. 25.

Sir Isaac Newton,
The Well House.

Mr Alderman
Ptolemy Tortoise

Request the pleasure of

Sir Isaac Newton's
Company at Dinner
on Dec. 25th
(to meet our friend Fisher)

R.S.V.P.

Mr. Alderman P. Tortoise,
Melon Pit,
South Border.

Dear Mr Alderman,
   I shall look forward to
dining with you on Dec. 25th.
It is an unexpected pleasure as
I thought you were asleep. No
doubt the melon pit is proof
against frost. I am nearly
frozen in the well house. Our
friend Fisher was taking mud
baths at the bottom of the
pond when I last met him.

       Yrs. faithfully,
         I. Newton

Ribby's Invitations

Mrs. Duchess,
Belle Green.

My Dear Duchess,
  If you are in, will you come
to tea this afternoon? but if
you are out I will put this in
the post & invite cousin
Tabitha Twitchit. There will be
a red herring, & the patty pans
are all locked up, do come.

Yr. aff. friend,
Ribby.

Mrs. Tabitha Twitchit,
Hill Top Farm.

Dear Cousin Tabitha,
   If you can leave your family
with safety I shall be much
pleased if you will take tea
with me this afternoon. There
will be muffins and crumpets
& a red herring. I have just
been to call on my friend
Duchess, she is away from
home.

       Yr. aff. cousin,
         Ribby.

Mrs. Ribstone Pippin,
Lakefield Cottage.

Dear Cousin Ribby,
  I shall be pleased to take tea
with you. I am glad that
Duchess is away from home. I
do not care for dogs. My son
Thomas is well, but he grows
out of all his clothes, and I
have other troubles.

    Yr. aff. cousin,
        Tabitha Twitchit.

Mrs. Ribstone Pippin,
Lakefield Cottage.

My dear Ribby,
   I am so sorry I was out, it
would have given me so much
pleasure to accept your kind
invitation. I had gone to a dog
show. I enjoyed it very much
but I am a little disappointed
that I did not take a prize and
I missed the red herring.

          Yr. aff. friend,
             Duchess.

Mr. Samuel
Whiskers'
Correspondence

To Samuel Rat,
High Barn.

Sir,

I hereby give you one day's notice to quit my barn & stables and byre, with your wife, children, grand children & great grand children to the latest generation.

signed: William Potatoes, farmer.

witness: Gilbert Cat & John Stoat-Ferret.

Farmer Potatoes,
The Priddings.

Sir,
I have opened a letter
addressed to one Samuel Rat.
If Samuel Rat means me, I
inform you I shall *not go*, and
you can't turn us out.

Yrs. etc.
Samuel Whiskers.

Mr. Obediah Rat,
Barley Mill.

Dear Friend Obediah,

Expect us—bag and baggage—at 9 o'clock in the morning. Am sorry to come upon you suddenly; but my landlord William Potatoes has given me one day's notice to quit. I am of opinion that it is not legal & I could sit till Candlemas because the notice is not addressed to my proper sur-name. *I* would stand up to William Potatoes, but my wife will not face John Stoat-Ferret, so we have decided on a midnight flitting as it is full-

moon. I think there are 96 of
us, but am not certain. Had it
been the May-day term we
could have gone to the Field
Drains, but it is out of the
question at this season.
Trusting that the meal bags
are full.

Yr. obliged friend,
Samuel Whiskers.

Sally Henny Penny's Invitations

(Private)
Master Tom Kitten,
Hill Top Farm.

Sally Henny Penny
at Home
at the Barn Door
Dec. 24th
Indian Corn and Dancing
Master T. Kitten,
Miss Moppet
&
Miss Mittens Kitten.

Miss Sally Henny Penny,
Barn Door.

Dear Henny,
    Me and Moppet and Mittens
will all come, if our Ma doesn't
catch us.

                T. Kitten.

The Puddle-Duck Family,
Farm Yard.

Sally Henny Penny
at Home
at the Barn Door
Dec. 24th
Indian Corn and Dancing
Mr. Drake Puddle-Duck
&
Mrs. Jemima
&
Mrs. Rebeccah

Miss Sally Henny Penny,
Barn Door.

Mr. Drake Puddle-Duck and
Mrs. Jemima accept with much
pleasure, but Mrs. Rebeccah is
laid up with a sore throat.

Rebeccah Puddle-
Duck's
Correspondence

Mrs. Ribstone Pippin,
Lakefield Cottage.

Dear Mrs. Ribby,
   Can you lend me a red
flannel petticoat to wear as a
comforter. I have laid up with
a sore throat and I do not
wish to call in Dr. Maggotty. It
is 12 inches long, a mustard
leaf is no use.

   Yr. sincere friend,
      Rebeccah Puddleduck.

Mrs. Rebeccah Puddleduck,
Farm Yard.

Dear Beccy,

I am sorry to hear of your
sore throat, but what can you
expect if you will stand on
your head in a pond? I will
bring the flannel petticoat &
some more head drops directly.

Yr. sincere friend,
Ribby.

The Birds'
Correspondence

Miss Jenny Wren,
The Nest,
Beech Hedge.

Dear Miss Jenny,

Will you accept a little cask of currant wine from your trusted friend Cock Robin! The carrier will leave it at the garden gate.

Cock Robin Esq.,
The Holly Bush.

Dear Cock Robin,
   I thank you kindly for the
little cask of currant wine. I
have worked a new little
scarlet waistcoat for you. Will
you dine with me on Christmas
day on the parlour window
sill?

                    Yr. aff. friend,
                    Jenny Wren.

Jack Sparrow,
The Eaves.

Dear Jack Sparrow,
   I have overheard that Jenny
Wren & Cock Robin are going
to eat their Christmas dinner
on the parlour window sill.
Lets all go and gobble up the
crumbs. Bring Dick Chaffinch
and I'll tell the Starlings.

        Yr. friend in mischief,
        Tom Titmouse.

The Flopsy Bunnies'
Correspondence

Miss M. Moller,
Caldecote Grange,
Biggleswade.

My dear Miss Moller,
   I am pleased to hear that
you like the F. Bunnies,
because some people do think
there has been too much
bunnies; and there is going to
be some more!
   My family will appear again
in the next book; and
Cottontail is put in because
you asked after her, which me
and Cottontail thanks you for
kind inquiries and
remembrance.

Yrs. respectful
Flopsy Bunny.

Dear Madam

My wife Mrs. Flopsy Bunny has replied to your inquiries, because Miss Potter will attend to nothing but hatching spring chickens; there is another hatch chirping this evening. And she is supposed to be doing a Book, about us and the Fox; but she does not get on; neither has she answered all her Xmas letters yet.

Yrs
B. Bunny.

Master John Hough,
88 Darenth Road,
N.W.

Dear Master John Hough,
   I and my Family (6) are
writing to you because Miss
Potter has got no stamps left
and she has got a cold, we
think Miss Potter is lazy. I
think you are a *fine big* boy;
my children are *small* rabbits
at present.

            Yrs. respectfully,
               Mrs. Flopsy Bunny.

Dear Master John Hough,
I wish you a Merry
Christmas! I am going to have
an apple for my Christmas
dinner & some celery tops. The
cabbages are all frosted but
there is lots of hay

Yrs. aff.
First Flopsy Bunny.

x x x x x x x

Dear Master John,
I wish you the same as my
eldest brother, and I am going
to have the same dinner.

Yrs. aff.
2nd. Flopsy Bunny.

x x x x x x x

Dear Master Hough,

I wish you the compliments of the Season. We have got new fur tippets for Christmas.

Yrs. aff.

 3rd. (Miss) F. Bunny.

x x x

Dear Master John,

I have not learned to rite prop perly.

Love from

 4th. (Miss) F. Bunny.

There are just a scribble and a few kisses from the 5th Miss F. Bunny; and a scribble and a few kisses 'with his love', from the 6th Master F. B.